More praise for
THE DAY THEY GAVE BABIES AWAY

"A story that is at its best when read aloud—to listeners of all ages. It deserves a place not far away from Dickens's *A Christmas Carol* on the family bookshelf."
        The Washington Star

"Its straight, unsentimental telling and its moving theme of courage is ageless. It's good to have it back again!"
        Publishers Weekly

❋

THE DAY
THEY GAVE
BABIES
AWAY

Dale Eunson

✳

BALLANTINE BOOKS · NEW YORK

Copyright © 1946, 1947, 1970, 1990 by Dale Eunson

All rights reserved under International and Pan-American Copyright Conventions. Published in the United States of America by Ballantine Books, a division of Random House, Inc., New York, and simultaneously in Canada by Random House of Canada Limited, Toronto.

This story originally appeared in *Cosmopolitan* magazine in a somewhat different form.

Library of Congress Catalog Card Number: 89-64437

ISBN 0-345-37250-6

This edition published by arrangement with New Chapter Press

Manufactured in the United States of America

First Ballantine Books Edition: December 1991

Illustrations: Phil Huling

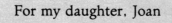
For my daughter, Joan

The Day They Gave Babies Away

*

MAMIE SAT ON THE FRONT PORCH
AND WATCHED ROBERT WORK IN THE
BOAT YARD.

YOU PROBABLY DON'T RE-member your grandfather at all, Joan. For the few years he was alive after you were born we lived in New York and he in California. You saw him only once, that summer we drove west when you were four years old. He thought you were wonderful. Which was right in character, since he thought all his children and his grandchil-dren were better than anybody else's.

1

THE DAY THEY GAVE BABIES AWAY

I have a precious mental picture of you sitting on his lap—he was eighty-three, still handsome, his hair silvery white, his features still rugged and strong, his black eyes dimmed a little by the memories and the confusions of things they had seen. And, of course, it is a moving picture because he is talking, spinning yarns he has spun for three-quarters of a century, telling tales of his boyhood, his young manhood, tales he had told me when I was your age and older: about the bear he met face to face in the Wisconsin woods the fall he was twelve, about the day he had all his teeth pulled by an itinerant dentist in the town square with the simple anaesthesia of a pint of rye whiskey, about the time when he was sheriff of Clark County and brought in an

2

insane killer single-handed. Papa, you see, was never one for false modesty. If he was the hero of most of his stories, why, hell's fire, that's the way he'd tell them because that's the way they'd happened.

His stories, the last ten or fifteen years of his life, had lost some of their vitality. He could not remember exactly when this and that happened, how old he was at the time, whether Al Rounds had a moustache or not. Things like that bothered him, slowed him up. He'd ramble, forget the point, sometimes need prompting to be set back on the track. "Jeezlum God," he'd say (his profanity was constant, picturesque, and strangely innocent), "I'm getting to be a forgetful old fool."

3

THE DAY THEY GAVE BABIES AWAY

I have told you most of his stories, Joan, but now here are your children, Dale, Marie, and John, and the grandchildren of my brother Bob and sisters Genevieve and Era, who never knew their most uncommon common ancestor, or had the privilege of sitting on his lap and toying with his fat Waltham watch while he hugged them and told his tales. So before I too forget, let me tell you young people one of them. His own. It is a Christmas story that he never thought all that remarkable.

"Hell's fire," he would say. "It was just something I promised my mother. I never went back on a promise." He was twelve years old at the time, and the time was 1868.

And one of these years in the twenty-first century I daresay you

4

THE DAY THEY GAVE BABIES AWAY

will be telling this story to your
own grandchildren. It can make
them stand a little straighter.

YOUR GREAT-GRANDFA-
ther was a sailor and a ship's car-
penter who was born on Fair Isle,
the southernmost and one of the
smallest of Scotland's Shetland Islands. His name was Robert
Strong Eunson and, as I discovered not long ago when I visited
Scotland, the name Eunson is as
commonplace in the Shetlands
and the Orkneys as Smith in
America. Robert married in 1855
and crossed the Atlantic with his

new wife, Mamie, during the spring of '56. There is no record of why they came, nor is there any need of an explanation. One does not ask why a Russian, a Korean, a Czech, a Guatemalan or a Cambodian deserts the harsh realities of his homeland for the dreams of a better world.

In Scotland, the land of the red-headed and the fair-haired, Robert and Mamie, with their black eyes and black hair, had been striking exceptions to the norm. Black Scots they were called. Nearly three centuries before, a galleon from the Spanish Armada had been sunk off the rugged coast of tiny Fair Isle, and Scottish sheep growers had rescued a number of the Spaniards, a fact that may account for the dark strain in some Scots.

☼

THE DAY THEY GAVE BABIES AWAY

Robert and Mamie headed straight for the heart of America, Chicago being the place where they first stopped to catch their breath and look about them. Mamie was six months pregnant, and they would need to find a home quickly. Robert, who had spent most of his savings for their passage, could waste little time in finding work.

He found it in a tiny town called Eureka on the Fox River in Wisconsin. Small boats were built there, launched onto the Fox, floated down to Lake Winnebago, and thence to Green Bay on Lake Michigan.

They moved into a two-room log house near the river, only a few steps from Robert's work. Mamie could sit on the porch, if she ever had the time, and watch him in the boat yard. He could straighten up from his bench occasionally and wave to her. They were very much in love, young and carefree.

The young couple made friends quickly, because they were that sort—warm, trusting, outgoing. They must have felt an urgency to put down roots in this new land so far from the island that had been their small sea-battered world, a place they had left knowing full well they would never see it again unless they struck it rich. This was beyond their dreams, for all they wanted was a home, enough to eat, neighbors to turn to in need, and, of course, each other.

On October 12, in the year 1856, their first child was born. They named him Robert for his father and his father's father, and from the first he was a lusty infant whose screams could be heard, when the windows were open, clear down to the shipyard and beyond. He was delivered by Mrs. Pugmeyer, the midwife who lived next door and who stayed with Mamie until she could be up and about her household tasks three days later.

Robbie, as they called him, was the spit and image of his father— noisy, roistering, good hearted, quick to anger, quicker to forgive. At the age of two he got into a brawl with a three-year-old from across the street, landed a lucky haymaker, and decked the older boy. The kid's name was John Bradley, and his father, a store-keeper, came blustering for revenge from Robert. Robert was reasonable, though glowing with pride, which must have been a little too obvious. At any rate, John's father demanded that Robbie be kept tied up so that he would not terrorize the neighborhood. Finally Robert had had about enough of this and swung on him. It was like-son-like-father that time. Robert helped Mr. Bradley to his feet and apologized, but he said Bradley had better keep young John out of the way because he'd be damned if he'd tie up any son of his. This was a free country, wasn't it?

Later that same day the Bradleys and the Eunsons looked out in the street and discovered Robbie and John playing peaceably together. John knew who was boss, and so did Robbie. And, to

12

THE DAY THEY GAVE BABIES AWAY

show that there were no hard feel-
ings, Mamie took her trade to the
Bradley store.

WELL, THE EUNSON FAMily grew considerably. Brothers and sisters for Robbie arrived at two-year intervals. First came Jimmie, who was a younger version of Robbie—the same black hair and piercing black eyes, but with a slightly mellower disposition. Jimmie didn't scream for what he wanted; he got his way by more diplomatic methods. Then there was Kirk, who was surprisingly tall even as a baby (the Eunsons had all been short, solid men). Robert said he must be a throwback to Mamie's grandfather, who was six foot two and built like a bean pole. Though endowed with enormous personal charm, Kirk was considered a little odd by the other members of the family, who were so much of a piece. He didn't like to fight, so Robbie always fought his battles for him. Robert thought Kirk might become a fiddler, and when he was six years old he made the boy a violin in the shipyard. (That's an instrument I should love to have seen and heard. Papa, of course, remembered it as being the most wondrous thing ever fashioned by the hand of man, and I'm sure that if love can be transmuted into tone, the songs it sang were sweet.)

THE DAY THEY GAVE BABIES AWAY

Then, as if to complement the trio of boys, the Eunsons brought forth three girls—Annabelle, Elizabeth, and Jane, all named for Mamie's sisters back home. All had the family's dark hair and dark eyes, and, strangely enough, they seemed to repeat the pattern of the boys in disposition and character. Annabelle was quick-tempered, quick-gaited. She never walked when she could run. She was her father's child—loving, tempestuous, flirting with the boys at four, her black pigtails flying in the breeze. Elizabeth was her mother's—quiet, affectionate, and protective. And Jane? She seems to have been the dreamer and romantic. Robert, who loved music, began to think of her as a pianist. He looked forward to the days when she and Kirk would

17

make music for him and Mamie and the neighbors to dance by. (Robert was a great one for the clog and hornpipe.) The arithmetic teacher, Mr. Skipworth, could play a little, and Robert hoped he might give Jane lessons when she was old enough. But he worried about how to get a piano. He was reconciled to the fact that he lacked the skill and materials to build one himself, though he had made everything else in the house—tables, chairs, and beds.

The Eunson family prospered a little, though it was along no quick road to riches. As soon as he could, Robert stopped selling his trade by the day and went into business for himself. He began to contract for small river and lake boats, hiring other men and working alongside them himself.

THE DAY THEY GAVE BABIES AWAY

He enlarged the house to accommodate the growing family. There were good times and lean times. An injury to his shoulder kept him out of the Civil War, and the war in turn kept him from the affluence that might have been his as there was little commerce and less shipbuilding on the inland waterways of the northern states until Lee surrendered.

Yet the family got along. The growing town pushed the forest back. Wisconsin was mostly timberland then, and it was during those years that the big loggers began to realize the fortune to be had for the mere felling and transporting of the tall maples and spruce and pine to the sawmills that mushroomed along the rivers and lakes. Winters, when the waterways were solid, the frozen silence of the forest was shattered by the rasp of the saw, the ring of the ax, and the crashing of the giants. And when the ice broke up, the rivers were clogged with the logs, dead and stripped of their limbs, rushing over the rapids, jamming the narrows, piling up before the dam sluice gates—there to be herded through for final disposition as siding, floors, supports, matches, furniture, fuel.

The Fox, idling through the Eunsons' front yard, was one of these rivers. In winter Robbie and his brother, Jim, would skate on it. They had to take turns, because there was only one pair of skates, but these were beauties—with turned-up toes and tiny bells that made music with each stride across the ice. In the spring they watched the logs glide past, watched the loggers with their peevees and cant hooks riding herd on them, cursing, roaring at their dangerous flock and at each other. And in the summer there were Robert's boats to help launch, the vegetable garden to tend, an occasional paper from Chicago to read, and once in a blue moon the mail from relatives in Scotland.

That was Robbie's small world for twelve years, physically a small world but always an exciting one, a world warm and full of the love he received and gave back double to his family and his friends.

IN THE SUMMER OF 1868 Kirk came down with diphtheria, an acute and extremely infectious disease that attacks the air passages of the throat. Before the development of an inoculation some twenty-five years later, it claimed the lives of many of its victims. As soon as Robert and Mamie realized the seriousness of Kirk's condition they held a family conference and decided they must get the rest of the children out of the house. Robert had a friend who owned a log cabin up in the woods, and Mamie said the only thing was for him to take the other five to the cabin and stay there until Kirk got well (she never admitted that Kirk might die). Robert argued that he was the one who should stay with the sick boy, but Mamie would have none of that. What did a man know about taking care of a young one? The boy needed his mother.

So Robbie and Jimmie and their three small sisters took to the woods with their father. For the girls it was all adventure, berrying in the underbrush, spotting a speckled fawn, finding strange and wonderful flowers. At night they watched the moon through the window as it crawled up and up the branches of trees, and they listened to the not-so-distant cries of wild animals, shivering and drawing close to each other, trying to guess what they were. One night they were sure they heard a bear prowling just outside the door.

But for Robbie and Jimmy the adventure was tempered by their concern for Kirk. Though they never said it out loud, they knew there was a chance their young brother could die. (Only three weeks earlier the body of John Bradley, the boy Robbie had knocked down years before, was carried to the little cemetery.) Once a day Robert walked to the edge of town, where Mrs. Pugmeyer met him with food and news of Kirk, and Robbie and Jim waited in the clearing around the cabin for him to return. They

25

could tell the instant they saw
their father whether or not Kirk
was still alive.

After the fifth trip to town,
Robert returned with a smile on
his face. The boys waited without
a word until he was beside them,
but of course they already knew.
It was quite a while before Robert
could find his voice, and when it
came it came with a roar, "By
God!" he cried. "The kid's going
to get well!" He kept saying "By
God!" over and over again, not
like a curse, but as if it were by
God's grace that the child had
survived. And then the tears came
quite unashamed, and he went
into the cabin and threw himself
down on one of the bunks. The
children crowded near the door—
they had never seen their father
cry before—but Robbie told them

to stay away. His father was tired and needed rest.

A few days later they returned to their home on the river. Kirk was up, pale and thin, his neck swathed in bandages. He felt terribly important and recounted in detail everything that had happened to him, but this soon palled on his brothers and sisters, who by now had decided that they had almost been eaten by a bear. Diphtheria was small potatoes beside such a terrifying possibility.

Three days later Robert, who had lost fifteen pounds during Kirk's illness, was stricken. This time there was no place for six children to go except Mrs. Pugmeyer's. She had no room, but she found floor space for them to sleep.

THE DAY THEY GAVE BABIES AWAY

They never saw their father again. On the fourth night of his illness he choked to death.

THE NEIGHBORS WERE kind, but kindness will go only so far toward clothing and feeding a family of seven. So Mamie worked, whenever there was work to be had. She took in sewing. When she could, she brought her work to the house; when she had to go out, Robbie or Jimmie stayed home from school to watch the younger children. Robbie wanted to go to work up in the woods that winter—he was twelve

THE DAY THEY GAVE BABIES AWAY

in October—but Mamie said an education was important and that he must complete the sixth grade before he quit school. With luck he would finish in the spring of '69, but there was no real certainty of it because he was not a very good student.

After the river froze in late November, he would put on his skates and travel up and down the river for miles to visit the nearest logging camps. These were in full swing every day of the week, and sometimes he could pick up a few pennies by acting as helper in the cook shanty or carrying hot soup to the men at noon. The men liked Robbie. He was small, about four foot nine, but he could lug a bucket of soup and sling thirty tin cups over his shoulder on a strap. It was on one of these trips that he met the bear on the trail. The boy and the bear stood for a long moment regarding each other. Then Robbie began to shake and his tin cups jangled. The bear turned and shambled off into the woods, and Robbie, after wiping the sweat off his brow, trudged on with the soup.

At age twelve, he had become the man of the house, though he did not look much like one. When there were problems Mamie consulted him. When Kirk broke his arm, Robbie held him while the doctor set it because Mamie could not stand to see a child of hers in pain. After Robert's death she had seemed to change. She did not cry after the first day or two, but there were times when she stood and stared—out the window or merely at the task before her.

THE DAY THEY GAVE BABIES AWAY

Perhaps she was thinking of Shetland and questioning their wisdom in leaving the islands. Had she been at home, countless relatives would have rallied to help her.

Mamie had always been thin and wiry, even though she was little more than five feet tall. But now she was no longer strong and her black eyes seemed to recede in her skull. Mrs. Pugmeyer told her she ought to eat more and try to put on some flesh, but Mamie had no appetite. When she tried to force food, it would not stay down. Besides, there were so many mouths to feed, and the children needed nourishment, she said, much more than she did. She was young enough, of course, to marry again, but there must have been very few men willing to take on a brood of six even if Ma-

ROBBIE BEGAN TO SHAKE AND HIS
TIN CUPS JANGLED.

mie would have considered it, which was doubtful.

It was on December 15 that the fever struck and Mamie lay down. "For a few minutes," she told Annabelle. "Your mamma feels a little tired." A batch of bread was in the oven, and it proved to be the last she was ever to bake, for she had typhoid, though she did not know this for three days. She thought it was an upset stomach and would not let Robbie call the doctor. When she grew delirious with fever, he took matters into his own hands and ran to fetch Dr. Delbert.

After he had examined her, the doctor called Robbie outside. "Your mamma is a sick woman," he said. "A very sick woman. Do you understand?"

Robbie said he guessed he did.

THE DAY THEY GAVE BABIES AWAY

"You mean she might not get well?"

"We can always hope," Dr. Delbert said, "but I want you to come a-running if there's any change. I'll be here every morning and every night to see her. But in the meantime you'd better get Mrs. Pugmeyer to come in and take over."

"She's gone," Robbie said. "She's down to Omro visiting her daughter until after New Year's."

"You ought to have somebody," the doctor said.

"We'll get along," Robbie said. "I'll stay home from school."

Dr. Delbert smiled. "You kinda like that, don't you, boy?"

"Yes, but not on account of Mamma."

"You're a good lad," the doctor said. He sighed and patted

him on the back. "Mrs. Delbert
will be over every now and then
to look in on you."

"Don't worry about us," Robbie said.

Mamie grew worse—and better—
and worse. She was delirious most
of the time, but there were peri-
ods of lucidity. These must have
been harrowing to her, for whenever she was herself the six children crowded into the room to say
hello. On the morning of December 23, as her brood was leaving,
she asked Robbie to remain.

She took his hands in hers.
They were hot and dry and her
eyes were fierce. He had to bend
close to hear her, for her tongue
was thick and her voice a rasp.
She told him she was going to
die. She said not to feel bad for
her, not to mourn her because

37

there wouldn't be time. There would be more important things for him to do. And then she told him what he was to do with the children. They were all nice, good children, she said, and he could get decent homes for them. Since the responsibility must be his, he was to decide where they were to be offered. And since they were such a large family, it would be better, she thought, if they were placed with families that had children of their own. Then they wouldn't be so lonesome for each other.

Robbie couldn't speak, but she had to know he understood, so she made him nod his head after each point.

"You watch out for them," she said. "You go and see to it as often as you can that they're taken care of."

He nodded his head.

And then she said, "Robbie, you get a good place for yourself. Promise me."

"I'll get along all right, Mamma. Don't you worry about me." Those were the only words he could say to her, but he had to say them. She let go of his hand and began once more to mumble unintelligibly. Robbie fled from the room and ran out into the woodshed.

Mamie died later that day.

After the funeral, Dr. and Mrs. Delbert and Mr. and Mrs. Bradley came back to the empty Eunson house with the children. They felt, with justification perhaps, that they were the most substantial and solid citizens among the friends of the Eunson family. The problem was, What to do with the children, and it was a big problem. But it could not be put off.

Kirk, Annabelle, Elizabeth, and Jane were sent outside to play while Robbie and Jimmie, who was ten, sat around the stove in the kitchen with the Delberts and the Bradleys. Dr. Delbert spoke first.

"You children will have to be put out for adoption," he said, "and I'm afraid we can't expect any one family to take on six youngsters."

Mrs. Delbert and Mrs. Bradley were dabbing at their eyes with their handkerchiefs, and muttering "poor little tykes, poor little motherless young 'uns." Robbie was dry-eyed, though his throat was full and he could not yet speak.

"Six is a lot," Mr. Bradley said.

THE DAY THEY GAVE BABIES AWAY

"Maybe the Owenses would take two. Faith and I could take on young Bob here in a pinch, I guess."

Young Bob. Nobody had ever called him that, and he liked the sound of it. Not just a kid. His father's son. And now Mr. Bradley, whose own son was dead, would take him on "in a pinch." Well, he'd see about that.

Mrs. Delbert said, "Our family's so large already. . ."

And Mrs. Bradley said, "Mrs. Pugmeyer's always been close to them. Do you suppose the town could hire her to take care of them? It'd sort of be like starting an orphanage. We need an orphanage. There's bound to be more cases like this."

The newly christened "young Bob" found his voice then. "You

all mean to be kind, I guess, but I'm the oldest and Mamma said I was to decide where we were to go."

"You?" Dr. Delbert was naturally surprised.

"That's right," young Bob said, not quite daring to meet the man's eyes. "And there's something I'd like. Tomorrow's Christmas. It'll probably be our last chance to be together on Christmas. Would you please go away now and leave us alone? And day after tomorrow we can make up our minds?"

The Delberts and the Bradleys looked at each other, and they seemed about to protest when Jimmie spoke up. "That's not very much to ask, is it?"

Dr. Delbert cleared his throat. "No, you're right, James. That's not very much to ask. Coming, Edith?''

So they left the children alone that night. There was plenty of food in the house, and after supper they huddled together. There were no Christmas stories, and no presents, which was odd, but perhaps the townspeople thought it not quite proper to give presents to children who had just been orphaned. Young Bob put the younger ones to sleep by telling them stories about the Shetland Islands and the days when Robert and Mamie were young, stories they had told him. He told them about the time when Robert, already engaged to Mamie, had sailed away in search of Sir John Franklin and his explorers, who had not been heard from since the day six years earlier when they set out to discover the Northwest Passage. And how Robert had been gone for three years and Mamie had put on mourning for him, thinking him dead, and how one afternoon Robert's ship had appeared on the horizon and next day Robert and Mamie were married. And he told them how the young couple had come to America so that their children—Robert and James and Kirk and Annabelle and Elizabeth and Jane— would have a chance for a better life. It was big talk for a twelve-year-old, much too big talk for the younger ones, but somehow he had to tell it while they were all together. He had to let them know that they were still going to have that chance.

So finally, one by one, their heads nodded and they went to

sleep, and only young Bob, as he now thought of himself, and Jimmie were awake. They talked until midnight, and they made a list on a paper bag, a list of the families in town that they thought would like children, be good to them, and bring them up as they would their own.

"We won't wait until day after tomorrow," Bob said.

"But you told Dr. Delbert you would," Jimmie said.

"I know that. But Mamma told me I was to decide. They won't let me. And tomorrow being Christmas, we ought to get just about anybody we want to take any of us in."

He was a little bit ashamed of himself for appealing to the sentiment of the season, but he knew what he was doing.

THE DAY THEY GAVE BABIES AWAY

Mr. Howard Tyler owned the livery stable. He had twelve horses, four teamsters, and half-a-dozen rigs—a surrey for weddings and outings, a hearse for funerals, and four buggies that could be fitted with runners in winter. He was, as they said in those days, well fixed. Young Bob had spent many hours at the stable, for he loved horses, and sometimes Mr. Tyler let him pump water into the troughs. Mrs. Tyler, already the mother of two boys, Howard Jr. and Bruce, was a leader in church doings and a great organizer.

The Tylers were ready to enjoy their Christmas dinner at one that afternoon. Mr. Tyler had just lifted his head from saying grace when there came a rather tentative knock on the kitchen door.

THE DAY THEY GAVE BABIES AWAY

Mrs. Tyler frowned and said, "Now who could that be? Folks should be at home enjoying their victuals this time of day," and went to the door. Two small children greeted her, a boy of twelve and a girl of six. She immediately recognized them as Eunson children, and she felt guilty. In the rush of preparing for Christmas she had neglected to do anything about them.

"Why, Robbie," she said, "I thought you'd be with the Bradleys or the Delberts. Come in, come in."

As she held the door for them she noticed that they both looked scrubbed and shining and were decked out in their Sunday best. The girl's hair was plaited and tied with two red bows that were not quite the same color as her stocking cap.

"I'm Annabelle," the child said, and young Bob said, "Yes, she's my sister Annabelle."

By this time they were in the dining room. The two boys stared at the visitors, but Mr. Tyler got to his feet and shook hands with them. "You'll have Christmas dinner with us," he said. "And don't argue. We won't take no, will we, Emma?"

"We certainly will not," Mrs. Tyler said.

"Begging your pardon, Mrs. Tyler, but I was wondering—that is Jimmie and I were wondering—if you didn't need a, a sort of sister, for Howie and Bruce. Annabelle here is a good little girl, and she'd be an awful help to you. She's—that is she was—learning to

45

sew and she can wipe dishes and she knows her ABC's.''

''A-b-c-d-e-f-g-h-'' Annabelle began.

Mrs. Tyler's mouth started to work in a very strange sort of way. Mr. Tyler coughed and turned his head. Howie, who was six, stared at Annabelle and said, ''What you got in that bundle?''

''I-j-k-l . . . My clothes,'' Annabelle said primly. ''M-n-o-p . . .''

And then Mrs. Tyler grasped her husband's hand and was staring into his eyes.

''Howard,'' she said. ''It's Christmas. We've got to—we've wanted a girl.''

''Mamma always said Annabelle was a good helper,'' young Bob put in.

And then Mr. Tyler kissed Mrs.

THE DAY THEY GAVE BABIES AWAY

Tyler right there before them all, and when he let her go she turned away and blew her nose while Mr. Tyler squatted down and took hold of Annabelle's shoulders. "Do you think you're going to like living at our house?" he asked. He was already unbuttoning her coat.

She did not answer because she was unbuckling her overshoes, but young Bob said, "Yes, Mr. Tyler. She'll like it a heap. She likes anybody that's good to her."

"We'll be good to her, Robbie," he said. "I guess you and I know each other."

"I know you, Mr. Tyler."

And so Annabelle was accounted for. Hereafter she would be Annabelle Tyler. She would live in comparative luxury, for the Tylers were to prosper and become important citizens of the state. But as young Bob left her there that Christmas Day all he could be sure of was that she would be well loved. And that was enough.

Meanwhile, Jimmie, leaving Kirk at home to take care of Jane, the baby, had hauled Elizabeth on his green sled to the Potters' house across the river. But the Potters were gone for the day, so it happened that young Bob ran into his brother and sister on the deserted Main Street in front of Mr. Potter's hardware and food store. Elizabeth was cold and fretful and her nose was running. The boys' plans had suffered a setback—they had not provided themselves with any alternate foster parents the night before. And so Elizabeth, whimpering on the sled, suddenly assumed the dimensions of a white elephant, a very dear but vexing one.

"What'll we do?" Jimmie asked. "She's getting blue. We can't keep her out much longer." And then his face brightened. "There's the Carters. They live close."

"He owns a saloon," young Bob said. "Mamma would hate that."

They agreed that this was true and began trudging aimlessly down the street and around the block. As long as they kept moving, Elizabeth was quiet. One would mention a name, only to have the other boy discard it. Then they saw a cutter with two fast bays trotting toward them. The boys looked at each other and nodded. Young Bob ran out in the street, waving his arms.

The horses came to a stop, snorting steam and pawing the snow. Inside the cutter, wrapped in a coonskin lap robe, were a middle-aged man and woman.

"Hello, Mr. and Mrs. Stevens," Young Bob said, "I was just coming to see you."

"You were?" the man said. "Mrs. Stevens and I have been over at your house. We wanted to see if there was anything we could do."

"There is. That is, it's quite a lot to ask, but I thought since you and Mrs. Stevens didn't have any children you might like to take Elizabeth. That's her," he said, pointing.

"That is she," Mr. Stevens

53

corrected. He was the principal of
the school.

"Take her," Mrs. Stevens said.

"You mean for us to . . . ?"

"Well, sort of—sort of adopt
her. She's only four years old but
she's bright for her age. She
doesn't look very pretty now but
you'd learn to like her. Mamma
and Papa did. Mamma never had
any favorites, but if she had any,
I guess Elizabeth would have been
the one. She's quiet."

The Stevenses had never been
able to have children of their own,
a disappointment they had borne
privately and a situation to which
they had adjusted publicly. Mr.
Stevens called his pupils "my
children" but was inclined to be
pompous with them and hold
them at a distance. The truth was
that he was afraid to show how

much he liked and needed them. Even now, he did not let his eyes rest on Elizabeth, but turned them to his wife. When he spoke his voice was almost stern.

"You wouldn't care to take on this burden, would you, Jess?"

"Wouldn't I just!" And with a bound she was out of the cutter and swooping Elizabeth into her arms. "Look, Frank," she said. "Her eyes are like yours."

Young Bob wanted to say, No, they weren't, they were just like his father's, but he was in awe of the Stevenses and kept his mouth shut. Schoolteachers and policemen and preachers were in a class by themselves, and you did not contradict them. So he said instead, "She's a little hard to understand at first. She's got a

55

Scottish burr, but you'll get used to it.''

"You bet we'll get used to it!" Mr. Stevens said with what seemed unnecessary emphasis. "You boys come and see us whenever you can."

"Whenever we can," young Bob said, and waved them off. He looked down at the empty green sled. They had had no chance to say goodbye to Elizabeth and he was just as glad.

He wanted to cry and he wanted to swear. He wanted to cry because the family was breaking up so fast, and he wanted to swear because the little girl had not even turned to look back at Jimmie and himself. She'd gone straight into Mrs. Stevens's arms as if she'd known her all her short

56

life, and he couldn't help but feel that this was disloyal to Mamma.

"Kids forget awful fast," Jimmie said as they walked along.

"Yeah," young Bob said, kicking at an icicle that had fallen from the striped pole before the barber shop. "Suppose she'll grow up to be a schoolteacher?"

WHEN THEY GOT HOME IT was about two-thirty. Kirk met them at the door with a wild look on his face. "Old Mrs. Runyon's in there," he whispered. "Says she's going to take Jane."

Now here was a problem. Old Mrs. Runyon had been a widow for twenty years. She wore nothing but black and carried a cane that she used to swipe at dogs that nipped at her heels. She had once crippled a collie pup and it had to

THE DAY THEY GAVE BABIES AWAY

be put away. She was said to be a miser and very rich, though nobody knew how much money she possessed. There were rumors she kept it hidden somewhere in her root cellar. So with some justification, perhaps, she had evolved into a town character used as a threat to frighten children into obedience. As long as young Bob and Jimmie could remember they'd heard the expression, "You better be good or ol' Runyon will get you."

And now here she was to "get" Jane. It must have taken no little courage to face her.

When young Bob walked into the house she had Jane on her lap. He said, "I'm sorry, Mrs. Runyon, but Jane's already promised."

"Who to?" she snapped.

THE DAY THEY GAVE BABIES AWAY

He floundered then. He and Jimmie had the Ellises, a young couple with a baby girl, in mind for Jane, but of course the Ellises had not yet been consulted. So he said, "Nobody you know."

"I know everybody in this town," Mrs. Runyon said.

He said the first thing that came into his head: "These folks don't live in this town. They're—they're way up in Berlin."

"I don't believe you," the old woman said. "Besides, by whose authority are these children being disposed of?"

"Mamma said I was to decide," he said, standing his ground.

"You! Why you're just a little boy!"

"Begging your pardon, Mrs. Runyon, but no, ma'am, I'm not.

THE DAY THEY GAVE BABIES AWAY

I'm Bob Eunson, the oldest one in our family.''

''We'll see about this,'' Mrs. Runyon said.

With that she put Jane back in her crib and marched out of the house swinging her cane. As soon as she was out of earshot, Bob called Jimmie and Kirk inside and explained what had happened. They didn't know what Mrs. Runyon might do, but they felt that they hadn't much time to finish the job.

''You take Kirk over to the Cramers,'' Bob told Jimmie. The Cramers had no children, but Mrs. Cramer did own a cello, which she was said to play very nicely. ''Tell them Kirk can fiddle pretty good.''

Kirk began to cry. ''I don't

"I DON'T BELIEVE YOU," SAID OLD
MRS. RUNYON. "YOU'RE JUST A
LITTLE BOY!"

want to go," he said. "I want to stay with you."

Bob had been afraid of this. Kirk was the soft one. So Bob thrust his fiddle into Kirk's arms and gave him a shove. "Get a move on, and don't be a crybaby. Annabelle and Elizabeth didn't cry. Who do you think you are?"

He pushed Kirk away from him, and Jimmie took him by the hand to lead him out the door. Young Bob stood in the middle of the room and for a minute the weight of what he was doing was too heavy for him. His knees collapsed under him, and he sat on the floor and beat the boards with his fists until they hurt and brought him to his senses. Then he got up and as fast as he could changed all of Jane's clothes and shook her into sweater, leggings,

65

and coat. She was delighted at the prospect of going somewhere and made no trouble. Before he was finished Jimmie returned.

"Did they take him?" Bob asked.

Jimmie nodded. "What are you going to do with Janey?" he asked.

"Take her up to Berlin."

"But that's twelve miles."

"I'll pull her up the river on our skates, and then bring them back to you—sometime."

"You going to stay up there?" Jimmie asked.

"I'm going to work," Bob said. "Round's camp is just five miles out of town."

"You can have the skates," Jimmie said after a moment. "The skates and my sled for your red sled. Fair enough?"

66

THE DAY THEY GAVE BABIES AWAY

The red sled had been Bob's
pride, but where he was going he
would not have much time for a
boy's sled. So he said, "Fair
enough." And then, "You talked
to the Raidens?"

"No," Jimmie said. "But I
don't have to. They'll take me in.
You know Mrs. Raiden's always
said she wished she had a boy like
me."

Yet there was something in Jimmie's voice that betrayed a slight
distaste for the Raidens, and Bob
heard it. "You like 'em all right,
don't you?" he asked.

"I like 'em all right," he admitted.

"Then what's the matter?"

"All those girls!" Jimmie said.
The Raidens had four daughters
ages seven to twelve. "I can just
hear them." His little boy voice

went into a ridiculous imitation of a falsetto. "This is our new brother, Jimmie. Ain't he cute?"

"Well, ain't you?" Bob said.

Then Jimmie swung on him, and caught him on the jaw. Bob was stunned but fought back while Jane looked on in wide-eyed excitement and approval. They tussled, grappled, and struck at each other until the room was a shambles and Bob had pinned Jimmie to the floor.

"Give up?" Bob panted.

"Give up," Jimmie gasped.

"Admit you're cute?"

"I'm cute," Jimmie gagged.

They both got to their feet and straightened their clothes. They didn't know why they had fought, but they were glad they had. For a few minutes, they were small boys again, small boys who had

63

fought for the reasons small boys fight. The scuffle had cleared the air and momentarily eased their burden.

And soon, all too soon, they were standing outside with Jane strapped to the green sled. This was the moment Bob had dreaded. He was afraid Jimmie would want to kiss him goodbye, but the younger boy seemed to realize that this was not the thing to do. So they stood staring at Jane, not daring to look at each other. And then Bob said, "You go first."

"You'll skate down once in a while?" Jimmie asked.

"Sure," Bob said. "Every chance I get. And see you don't start to wearing dresses with all those girls around."

"You shut up!" Jimmie said.

THE DAY THEY GAVE BABIES AWAY

With that he turned and, pulling the bright red sled, walked away. Bob was afraid Jimmie might look back and see him, so he pulled Jane's sled behind the woodshed and peered out around the corner as his brother's figure grew smaller and smaller and finally disappeared behind Mrs. Pugmeyer's green picket fence.

As soon as he felt strong enough, Bob walked down to the river and put on his skates. Pulling a sled, it would take him three hours to make Berlin, and it would be dark by then. But the sky was clear and already the moon was in the eastern sky, though the sun still shone in the west.

Part of the way Jane slept, lulled by the motion of the sled. Once she cried, and he stopped and held her, wiping her cheeks and nose with the red mittens Mamie had knit for him. When she was quiet again he put her back on the sled and tucked the blanket around her. Slowly, mile after mile, the leafless trees slid past. Then it was dark, and the woods held shadows that seemed to move as Bob moved, so that for the last few miles he kept his eyes straight ahead while his legs pumped steadily and the exertion kept him warm. Each push, he reminded himself, removed them that much farther from the menace of Mrs. Runyon.

At last there were feeble lights in a cluster of houses along the river. They passed Al Rounds's sawmill, which would be silent till the spring thaw floated green timber down the Fox. They skated through a group of skaters who scarcely paused to notice the small boy with the baby on his sled. And a few moments later he saw a house with Christmas-tree candles winking at the front window. He came to a stop before it and gave it a silent inspection. If there was a tree there would be children, he thought. The house was not so very large. The people who lived there would not have a great deal of money. Therefore, his thoughts ran, it would be a small sacrifice to have a tree with candles. They must love their children.

So he took off his skates, lifted the sleeping Jane in his arms, climbed the steps onto the porch, and knocked at the door.

A plump woman with a green shawl over her shoulders, her dark

72

hair gathered in a knot low on her neck, opened the door. Instantly three children peered around her skirts. Bob heard her say, as if from a distance, "Well, for mercy's sakes. What have we here?"

And he heard himself say, "I'm Bob Eunson from down in Eureka. And please, ma'am, I was wondering if you'd like to have a baby."

I'M ASHAMED TO ADMIT it," your grandfather said when he told me this story, "but I fainted. Yes sir, plumb fainted dead away."

Yes, that was what your great-grandfather did that Christmas when he was twelve years old. And when Jane was safe in the hands of the Clareys, he said goodbye and walked up to the Rounds camp in the woods, where he became a helper, and later a logger in his own right.

THE DAY THEY GAVE BABIES AWAY

He always kept tabs on his brothers and sisters, most of whom turned out remarkably well. As they grew up, though, each one took on characteristics and absorbed points of view of his or her foster parents. They are all gone now, but I saw them, all but one, when I was young, and no one could doubt they were Eunsons—"Black Scots" with black hair and flashing black eyes. To me there was always something poignant in their concern and love for one another. Scattered as they were, they still held on to a sense of family.

When I knew Aunt Annabelle, she had become a great dowager with a home in California and one in Chicago. She ruled her children with an iron hand. Aunt Eliza-

76

WHEN JANE WAS SAFELY IN THE
HANDS OF THE CLAREYS, HE SAID
GOODBYE.

THE DAY THEY GAVE BABIES AWAY

beth indeed taught school, then
married, had two children, and,
after her husband died, became
the housemother at a girls'
school.

Jane never married. She gave
music lessons—voice—and herself
possessed a small, sweet con-
tralto. She, of course, had no
memory of that evening's ride on
the sled to her new home, but she
and Papa were always very close.
She used to come to our house
when I was small, and I can re-
member her sitting at the piano
singing "In the Gloaming," and
then breaking into "The Irish
Washerwoman." Papa would leap
to his feet and launch into a real
hoedown and make the furniture
jump.

Uncle Jim became a successful
lawyer in Wisconsin, married and

had three children. He and Papa wrote each other regularly once a month for as long as they both were alive.

Kirk was the only tragedy of the six. Life was too much of a struggle for him and he "took to drink," as Papa used to say. He died mysteriously when he was only twenty-five.

And that's about the end of the story. Your grandfather's life, at least in his own estimation, was a happy one. He worked until he was almost eighty.

After my mother died, when I was fifteen months old, he married again. He had seven children, three of whom died as infants. He knew poverty and success. It was a life of ups and downs, but in the downs he used to say, ''They can't lick a tough old nut like me.''

And they never did. Nobody ever did.

ABOUT THE AUTHOR

Dale Eunson has been a magazine editor, has written for radio and television, and has published two other books: *Up on the Rim*, a historical narrative of old Montana, and *Philip's Chair*, a novel. He lives in Santa Barbara, California.